This book is for my daughter, Amber Arnaktauyok.
—G.A.

For my little monster, Mia-Laure.
—N.C.

Those That Cause Fear

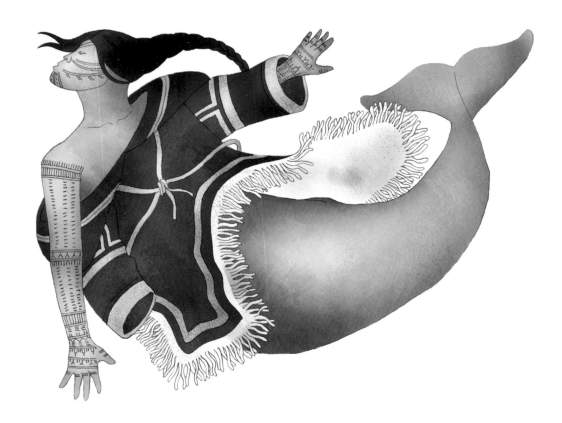

By Neil Christopher · Illustrated by Germaine Arnaktauyok

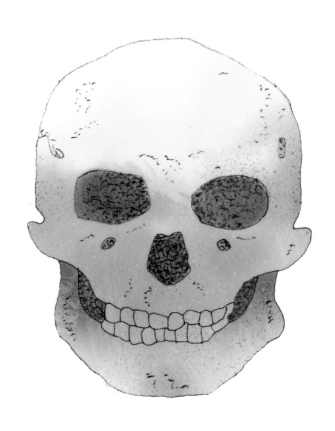

Table of Contents

Arctic Monsters

Try to imagine the dangers of living in the Arctic—what comes to mind? Did you think about the winter blizzards that bring powerful winds and blinding snow? It is true that blizzards are dangerous, as you can easily lose your way if you are not careful. Did you think of the dangers of travelling on the sea ice? It is true that the sea ice can shift and break, and can take people far out to sea away from their homes. Perhaps you imagined the huge animals, like polar bears or wolves? You would be correct, as these animals are large and strong, and need to be respected at all times.

But this book is not about those dangers. This book is about the dangers that lurk in the northern darkness and in the remote places of the Arctic. As you turn the pages of this book, you will be introduced to the things that go bump in the Arctic nights. This book is about Arctic monsters!

If you listen to hunters and elders telling stories about the North, you will find that some of the stories make reference to strange things that have been encountered on the tundra or sea ice.

I have spent years listening to these old stories, and researching the journals of Arctic explorers from long ago. I have gathered this information and presented some of it here in this book for those who are drawn to the mysterious things of the world.

An important thing to note is that some of the beings and creatures discussed in this book are said to have existed long ago and are no longer present in the world. But many of them are thought to still be out on the land, hiding and waiting for an unsuspecting person to wander close. So, sit back and get ready to meet the giants, cruel ogresses, supernatural creatures, beautiful sea people, and strange beings that inhabit the hidden world of the Arctic.

Amautalik

Those who wander the inland tundra, far away from the seacoast, should be watchful for a dangerous giant called an *amautalik*. An amautalik is an ancient ogress, both large and cruel, who wanders the tundra looking for children and lost travellers. These beings resemble large, monstrous women. They either wear an *amauti*—a parka used for carrying children—made of thick walrus skin, or they carry a basket made of driftwood, bones, and antler, lashed together with rotting seaweed. When people are caught, the amautalik will place its victims in the amauti's pouch or in the basket it carries to steal them away.

Dog Children

Those who hear the howls of dogs as they travel through remote regions of the North, beware! These sounds might not be the calls of sled dogs. They could be the calls of dangerous creatures that are part dog and part human.

Inuit elders tell the ancient story of a woman who was tricked into marrying a land spirit. Eventually she became pregnant, and gave birth to children that were a mixture of dog and human—the dog children! These dog children grew quickly and became very dangerous. In some regions of the Arctic, they say these dog children still wander the tundra looking for lone travellers and people who have lost their way.

Palraijuq

When travelling in the Western Arctic, you need to take care near rivers, ponds, and lakes, as these places are the habitat of the *palraijuq*. At one time, these aquatic monsters were common, but now there are very few left. The palraijuq is a large, reptilian creature with a long snakelike body that possesses six legs. This creature uses the water to hide itself. It is said that a palraijuq can lie motionless underwater for days while it waits for an animal or human to come to the water's edge for a drink. Once its prey is close, the palraijuq will leap out of the water, grabbing its victim in its huge mouth filled with hundreds of sharp teeth. Then the palraijuq will drag what it has caught underwater to drown it.

Earth Children

Imagine what the North was like a long time ago. Many things were different back then. If we listen to Inuit storytellers, we will learn that there were very few Inuit living on the land in those times. But those ancient days were a time of magic, and we are told that the land gave birth to children. These children were found on the ground and were adopted by the people who happened upon them. These children were sometimes called *nunamiinngaaqtut*, a word meaning "from the land." The earth children helped Inuit increase in number. They were just like any other human beings, but with a deeper connection to the land.

Iqallijuq

If you travel across the tundra, you will likely encounter many rivers and streams that weave across the land on their way to the sea. These waters are often rich with fish. Old stories tell us that these fish were the creation of a huge man and his magic axe. Inuit folktales tell us that this being was large and extremely ugly. It is said that he chopped old driftwood with his magical stone axe. With each strike from this axe, wood splinters would be thrown into the water. As soon as these pieces of wood touched the water, they were transformed into the char that are so common in the North. Because of this, the man is sometimes called *Iqallijuq*, meaning "Father of Char." It is because of this huge man that Arctic lakes and rivers are filled with fish.

Travellers beware: although this huge being did the North a great service by creating the fish that feed so many northerners, he is to be avoided. The old stories tell us that he is ashamed of his ugly appearance, and will use his axe to harm anyone who might see him.

Giant Fish

Have you ever gone fishing in a lake? Well, in the North, this can sometimes be dangerous! In remote Arctic lakes, it is said that codfish can sometimes grow to huge sizes. You will hear many storytellers from different regions mention these giant fish. It is said that they can grow large enough to swallow ducks and geese, and the largest of the giant codfish can even catch a caribou or a human that has fallen into the water!

Inukpasugjuk

Have you ever imagined seeing a giant? Do you think you would be scared? If you are lucky, you might encounter *Inukpasugjuk* and his adopted son. We are told that Inukpasugjuk was a kind giant. When travelling, Inukpasugjuk could step over mountains and wander far out into the sea. Even huge polar bears looked tiny to this giant, and he would often mistake them for little foxes.

Inukpasarjujuk

Imagine encountering a giant fishing by the seacoast. Can you guess what sea creature would be large enough to interest a giant?

On Baffin Island, in the region of Cumberland Sound, there lived a huge female giant called *Inukpasarjujuk*. This giant was so large that she would mistake bowhead whales for little fish. This giant would spend her days fishing for bowhead whales, and the smaller whales, like beluga and narwhal. We are told she could swallow the smaller whales in one bite!

Battling Giants

Imagine what it must have been like to see two great giants fighting. What do you think it would have sounded like to hear them yelling and falling to the ground?

Long ago, there were many great giants in the Arctic. These huge beings were incredibly strong and had little to fear in this world. However, elders tell us that these giants often did not get along with each other. When two giants met, it was quite common for these encounters to end in a deadly fight. Some people say that these fights are why there are very few giants left in the world.

Sleeping Giants

Have you ever been walking and come across a hill or mountain with no other mountains or hills around it?

We are told that when the great giants became tired, they would sometimes fall into a very deep sleep. If this happened, the giant might not wake up for centuries. After several years of not moving, dirt would settle on the giant, and plants would start to grow. Eventually the giant would look like a mountain, and people would never know that there was a giant sleeping beneath the plants. It is said that some of the hills and mountains in the Arctic are in fact sleeping giants!

Amarujjuat

Wolves can be very large, especially in northern regions of the world. However, there are magical wolves that live in the far North that are larger than any wolf you can imagine.

Across the Arctic, and especially in Greenland, there live giant wolves called the *amarujjuat*. These are mystical animals that possess great power and size, but also ancient magic. Amarujjuat are uncommonly wise, and have knowledge of many ancient things.

Akla Inua

In the North, you might encounter beings that look like people, but that are really the spirits of ancient animals.

Long ago, the people of the North would bury their dead under piles of stones. It is said that sometimes very strong beings would dig up these graves in search of an easy meal. These particular beings were sometimes referred to as *akla inua*—a grizzly bear in human form. These bearlike ogres walked on two legs, like a human being, but they were huge in size, with large claws and teeth, and their bodies were covered in hair.

Kajjait

Inuit have many rules to ensure that animals are respected, especially when hunting. If these rules are broken, there are often serious consequences. When the meat of a hunted animal is not used properly, or the meat is allowed to spoil, the animal's spirit could become angry. That is how the *kajjait* are said to have been created.

The descriptions of kajjait differ from region to region, but generally the kajjait are said to look like wolves, but they are skinnier, with larger heads. The kajjait are sometimes called the cursed wolves or the famished wolves, as these creatures are cursed with a constant hunger. It does not matter how much the kajjait eat; they will never be full. So, these creatures are constantly moving across the tundra looking for food. The kajjait are so hungry that they will even attack others in their own pack if they smell blood on them.

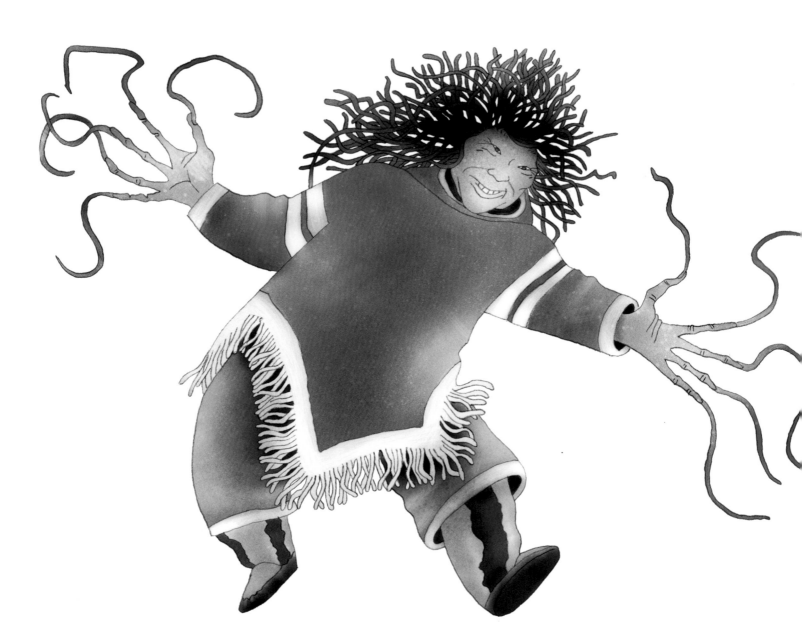

Mahahaa

If you are alone on the land in the winter, you need to watch out for a creature called *Mahahaa*. Mahahaa is a cruel being that is unaffected by wind or cold. It travels across the Arctic in the winter, looking for people who are alone and vulnerable. This creature has been described as a little being, with ice-blue eyes, and long, messy hair. Mahahaa has long, sharp fingernails, and a crazy smile filled with awful teeth. Mahahaa is always giggling. If this creature catches a person, it will tickle him or her to death!

Nuliajuk

Have you ever wondered why the Arctic seas have so many seals? We are told that this is because of one person—*Nuliajuk*. Nuliajuk is the mother of the sea animals.

Nuliajuk was once a beautiful woman who did not want to get married. However, a bird spirit tricked her into marrying him and she became his captive on an island of birds far away in the ocean. Eventually, Nuliajuk's father paddled to this island and tried to save his daughter. But, when the bird spirit learned of Nuliajuk's escape, he summoned a powerful storm to capsize the father's boat. Nuliajuk's father was afraid of the bird spirit, so he threw Nuliajuk into the ocean. But Nuliajuk held on to the side of her father's boat. Nuliajuk's father was so afraid of the bird spirit that he cut off Nuliajuk's fingers so she could no longer hold on to the boat. Nuliajuk sank to the bottom of the sea.

Ancient magic then transformed her cut fingers into the many sea animals that Inuit hunt, and she was given power over these animals and many other things. Now, people must be careful not to insult Nuliajuk, as she is always watching to make sure people respect animals, the sea, and the land.

Qallupilluk

If you are walking along an Arctic coast in the spring, you might hear something knocking under the ice, and you may even hear strange "glub-glub" sounds. These noises could mean that a *qallupilluk* is nearby.

The *qallupilluit* have large noses, and webbed hands and feet. A qallupilluk usually wears an amauti made of eider duck feathers. Beware of the qallupilluit in the spring, when the sea ice starts to break apart. These creatures wait underwater for children to play on the broken ice. Once a child gets close to the ice edge, the qallupilluk will grab him or her, and pull the child into the water. Once the child is in the water, the qallupilluk will trap him or her in the pouch of its amauti and take the child deep underwater. Some people say these creatures take children to be their pets, and keep the children on leashes made of seaweed.

Aasivak

In the summer, if find yourself boating in the northern seas and come across a small island with a strange dwelling on it, beware!

In the Arctic, there are many strange beings that choose to live far away from people, on remote islands. One of these beings is *Aasivak*, who appears as a strange-looking old woman with a huge *ulu*. Aasivak is actually an ancient spider that can take on human form. And, like a spider, this being will try to lure you into her home where you will be trapped. It is said that her ulu is a dangerous weapon that possesses powerful magic.

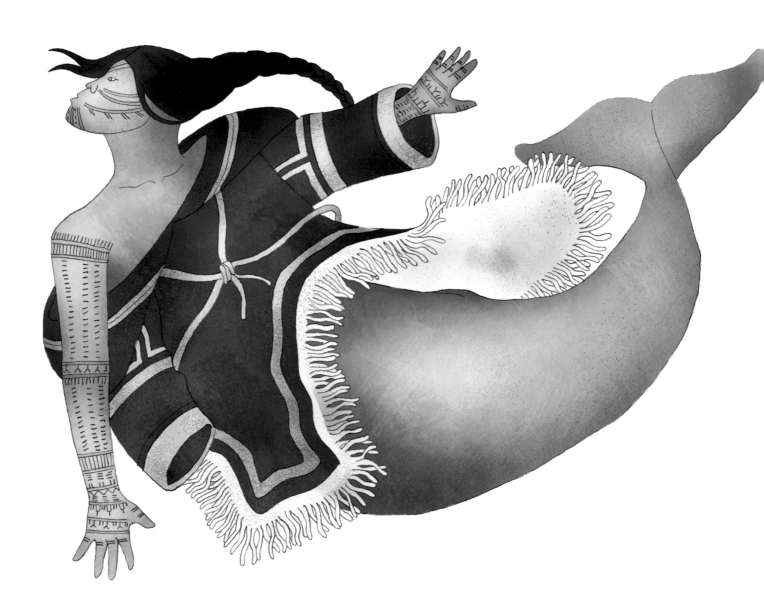

Taliillajuut

The Arctic Ocean is dark, cold, and mysterious. If you spend a lot of time boating in the Arctic seas, you might encounter a *taliillajuuq*. The explorers and Inuit hunters who have travelled these waters have shared many stories about beings and creatures that they have encountered on their trips. One being that is often talked about is the taliillajuuq. These marine beings look like humans from the waist up, but the bottom halves of their bodies are described as similar to the tail of a beluga whale. Female *taliillajuut* seem to be more common, and more approachable. They are described as having a beautiful appearance, with very long, black hair, and pale skin. On rare occasions, the male of this species is encountered. They are said to be cautious and distrustful of humans.

It is not known if the taliillajuut are friendly or dangerous. Some say they are kind and helpful, while others have stories of these beings leading boats to dangerous places.

Tuniit

Did you know that there were people living in the Eastern Arctic before Inuit arrived here?

Many, many years ago, when Inuit first arrived in the far North, they found the land already inhabited by a people they called the *Tuniit*. According to the oral history of Inuit, Tuniit were larger and much stronger than Inuit. They would build their houses out of large rocks that normal humans could not lift. It is said that a Tuniit hunter could hunt and carry a walrus without any help. For people who have seen a walrus, you know that no human alive today possesses enough strength to do that. It is said that the Tuniit showed the Inuit many things that helped them survive in the North. *Inuksuit*—stone markers used by Inuit today—were said to first be used by the Tuniit.

Nanurluk

Can you imagine travelling in a small boat and meeting a giant polar bear in the sea?

According to Inuit oral history, there is a type of polar bear that grows as large as an iceberg. This kind of bear is called a *nanurluk*, and it can become so large that it needs to spend most of its life in the sea. The weight of an adult nanurluk is so great that it cannot walk on land for very long without becoming tired. If a nanurluk does come onto land, it usually stays close to the coast, so it can slide back into the sea whenever it needs to. We are told that these monstrous bears have been known to attack hunters in their boats, or even villages along the coasts. It is almost impossible for Inuit to kill a nanurluk, because its fur is so thick and filled with ice that spears and arrows cannot penetrate it.

Traditional stories tell us that Inukpasugjuk and the other great giants loved to hunt the *nanurluit*. These giant bears were the only animals that could offer the giants an exciting hunt. So, over the years, the number of nanurluit has decreased. Some people say nanurluit are extinct, while others believe there are a few left in the remote regions of the Arctic, were people seldom travel.

Final Thoughts

There are still places in our world that have not been tamed, and the lands to the far North are just such places. Up here, where the winters are cold, dark, and long, there is still magic hidden away from the modern world. You will not find a travel guide or a map that will warn of the hidden things contained in this book. For that information, you need to study Inuit oral history and talk to the people who have lived in the Arctic for generations.

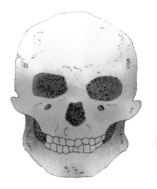

Inuktitut
Pronunciation Guide

Aasivak	aa-see-vac	nanurluk	na-nur-look
akla Inua	ak-la ee-new-a	nanurluit	na-nor-loo-weet
amarujjuat	a-ma-ru-jew-at	Nuliajuk	new-lee-a-yuk
amautalik	a-mow-ta-lik	nunamiinngaaqtut	new-na-men-ga-toot
amauti	a-mow-tee	palraijuq	pile-ray-yuk
Inukpasugjuk	ee-nok-pa-sew-yok	qallupilluk	ka-loo-peel-look
Inukpasarjujuk	ee-nok-pa-sar-yo-yok	qallupilluit	ka-loo-peel-loo-weet
inuksuit	in-uk-su-weet	taliillajuuq	ta-lee-la-yuk
Iqallijuq	ee-kal-li-yok	taliillajuut	ta-lee-la-yut
kajjait	ka-yah-t	Tuniit	to-neat
Mahahaa	ma-ha-haa	ulu	oo-loo

Published by Inhabit Media Inc.
www.inhabitmedia.com

Inhabit Media Inc. (Iqaluit) P.O. Box 11125, Iqaluit, Nunavut, X0A 1H0
(Toronto) 191 Eglinton Ave. East, Suite 301, Toronto, Ontario, M4P 1K1

Edited by: Louise Flaherty and Kelly Ward
Written by: Neil Christopher
Illustrated by: Germaine Arnaktauyok
Digital colours by: Jonathan Wright

Design and layout copyright © 2016 by Inhabit Media Inc.
Text copyright © 2016 by Neil Christopher
Illustrations by Germaine Arnaktauyok copyright © 2016 Inhabit Media Inc.

We acknowledge the support of the Canada Council for the Arts for our publishing program.

We acknowledge the support of the Government of Canada
through the Department of Canadian Heritage Canada Book Fund program.

Printed in Canada

Canadian Heritage Patrimoine canadien   Canada   Canada Council for the Arts   Conseil des Arts du Canada

Library and Archives Canada Cataloguing in Publication

Christopher, Neil, 1972-, author
Those that cause fear / by Neil Christopher ; illustrated
by Germaine Arnaktauyok.

ISBN 978-1-77227-085-3 (hardback)

1. Inuit mythology--Canada--Juvenile literature.
2. Monsters--Canada--Juvenile literature. I. Arnaktauyok,
Germaine, illustrator II. Title.

E99.E7C5471 2016   j392.2089'9712   C2017-901374-2